THE INTERVIEW

ALSO BY THIS AUTHOR

- YOUR LIVES JOURNEY BELIEFS

- A LOVE HATE RELATIONSHIP
  Between SNOWBELL AND DAISY

- 'ROSE' POSTCARDS AND THOUGHTS
  FROM A BEAUTIFUL PIG

- A CHRONICLE OF VERSES AND
  ECHOS

THE INTERVIEW

JACQUELINE MARY MASCIOTTI

To order additional copies of this book, contact:
Xlibris
1-800-455-039
www.Xlibris.com.au
Orders@Xlibris.com.au
731829

CONTENTS

DEDICATIONS

It gives me, my humble pleasure, to thank all the people I have known. Who have given voluntarily their support and encouragement in putting together a very special gift of mine, and by giving me the chance to share this book, of past and present lifetime memories!

I think that, as always I can illustrate the meaning of 'Never forget to belief in yourself; because no one will give this a second thought only you,' and you are the one that needs this vital thought, justifying a single word is what is needed, and that is "you."

A DOCUMENTED CONVERSATION

This 'Documented Interview' is a conversation taken between two people that captures episodes, nothing special or unusual but, perhaps it conveys in detail, flashbacks and occurrences that developed some direction of choices throughout a single lifetime.

It includes dedicated passion, happiness, and sadness, not to mention challenges, all combined, and of course not forgetting all the risks taken to achieve the fundamental goal of successful achievements.

- **It's like a tree that has been uprooted from its foundation and restored to a better place from adversity to enjoyment, and living in the environment suited by the tree in itself, an amazing part of pure nature that has taken place.**

Therressa Bouques, is a professional Journalist, and, Writer, who is currently working for a large International Magazine Company, called "The

Facts and Fiction Articles.' This is conducted by undertaking interviews from diverse people. Therressa Bouques is always motivated and intrigued by exploring people's past and current lives and writing about their adventures and how they became famous or successful in their own generation lifetime.

However, she is reaching a period in her own life that does not satisfy, not to mention the very thought of retirement, at least not at the moment, on the other hand she wants to reflect back on the pathways and directions she took from an early age in her choice of career, to her recent contentment in today's natural environment.

In order to do that, she can depict in detail these pathways by allowing a special friend called Millardd Myle, who is also a well known Journalist, but of a different type, as he is a Television Broadcaster and Journalist. He also records and interviews many variety of celebrities, to be screened on a national scale through Television Documentary shows.

He is devoted, and of course takes great pride in taking part in these interviews with prominent people and, to provide interesting reviews to the public audiences. At this point he chooses to interview and look deeper into the past and present realities that took place in Therressa Bouques life time.

He takes a journey through Therressa Bouques as a Journalist, in her choice of career and preference from other interesting options that would mark an astonishing and gratification of her life.

Therressa Bouques justifies that it's like a recipe that has not yet been sampled out or tasted, perhaps better still, it has not had the privilege of others to enjoy the flavour of privileged circumstances between mistakes, risks, and successes passed on to others that are so transparent in their own way of thinking.

Therressa starts thinking now, why she accepted to have this documented interview with Millardd, and should she have declined this opportunity, and yet all of the retained information gives way to the thoughts and quandary that took place years gone by in my life. I am also very fortunate to even recollect or even muse over these moments and, as normal when I end my day in the current company I am working for, it gives me great satisfaction to know that I have accomplished something constructive throughout the day.

I always have a positive mind and look forward to the next day at work with all the challenges it will bring to me.

This documented interview will capture moments, or flashbacks taken through the past as I remember it; however, Millardd mentions that it will take several sessions to accomplish his own satisfaction as to the selection and purpose of this interview with Therressa Bouques. It is not just the documented interview side of recording but, it will be broadcasted on television shows scheduled in the coming weeks from a large communication network company.

Millardd knows that it will take some effort, however, it will be valuable as she is known to have had a very interesting life, and I am sure that reflections will have cause to flow out as clearly and precisely, with passion. What a true professional, by any sense of the word.

Millardd also mentions, that often most people would like to write down their own adventures, experiences and reflect on all sorts of successes and mistakes, such as risks and opportunities either in use or left behind for fear of disappointment. However it needs endurance and strength to make the effort that is why he decided on Therressa Bouques as his candidate, because she has all of the qualities of a victorious Journalist and Writer.

- *He can't wait to get started!*

Therressa Bouques takes up the challenge of Millardd's documented interview and shares her past and current journey with him; and, also believes that perhaps it might relate to some of the audiences own voyage throughout their life time encounters.

- *Hence, Therressa, let's embark on your wonderful journey shall we?*

As they make their way into Millardd's studio, they begin to make themselves quite comfortable.

The surroundings are quite conducive to the atmosphere and the conditions required in making this documented conversation interview adaptable at any time. Therressa begins to relax as she is peering out of the window to see down below people in the streets going about their own business whether, shopping or going to work, she feels ready and happy for this opportunity.

I suppose the obvious first inquiry from Millardd would be to start asking Therressa Bouques about, why, want, and when she chose to become a Journalist including a career as a Writer?

- *She gives a great deal of thought to her appropriate responses as we begin this intriguing journey;*

Therressa requests that she will need to break up these definite inquiries, perhaps initially with the 'want' to put together and formulate a foundation of the journey that took place over a period of time.

It really materialized by accident a long time ago perhaps maybe twenty five or even thirty years ago at an early age. Maybe it was a driven force within me to embark on the unknown adventures!

My love and aspiration of reading and writing was paramount to me in all aspects of documenting and research findings about other people. I knew from an early age that I had a high-quality of listening skills and for that reason I utilized my efforts through my own imagination to succeed in any choice of career that gave me interest or stimulation within a field of listening skills.

The career in Journalism was opening doors of opportunities for me. I took notice of even examining the possibility of what I intended to write about. It became a natural source of communication for me to report on such recordings that, I composed and collected all information that might have taken place, such as interviewing celebrity models or even with corporate executives.

- *But, excuse me Therressa, was it all work and no play as the saying goes, did you enjoy and have fun with this type of work?*

- *So for you, it did become exiting!*

Oh yes indeed both, everyday was filled with various situations or circumstances even the overload on deadlines to keep up with, however, there could be some delays in meeting these deadlines, perhaps technology was a culprit or a missing line from an interview, worst of all would be the misinterpretations of the person you were interviewing and documenting issues about within an article.

I have always had the philosophy of 'get up and go attitude' whenever a certain task or situation occurs for me to concentrate on the importance and result of the outcome.

Subsequently, Millardd you asked me the 'when' it happened, as mentioned it was purely by accident. One of my colleagues within the accounting department required me to document and report on a financial yearly budget. A very important piece of information needed to be analyzed and presented to a 'Board of Directors', to establish the company's viability and, to embark on further projects in the upcoming future.

It took me months to research and analyze this data as, I had not only to gather past financial data but, to correlate this information from each staff member in the accounting and financial departments. Finally I was able to analyze and conclude my report and give a briefing of the outcomes by preparing presentations.

To my surprise everyone was delighted at the results, even though they showed negative and positive outcomes but, because of the succinct approach that I took within my report and presentation it became clear to them without any complexities a good effort.

As a result of this I was encouraged to continue with this approach and at the same time I was given an opportunity to transfer to the Journalism department.

At first it seemed a little bit scary leaving my comfort zone as they say but, I was ambitious and I thought "Why Not," I will give it a try and if it doesn't work out I will go back to my old boring department in finance. I mention being boring even although in reality it wasn't, but looking at figures, numbers all day long it seemed endless and non productive or challenging for me.

I also like to work under pressure with a powerful stride of tenacity and confidence that has been built up from discipline and courage over the years from my family background.

- *Millardd continues and allows Therressa to start thinking about the past and the whole journey that took her in this direction as a professional Journalist and Writer.*

Therressa begins where it all began and says, "It seems such a long time ago," perhaps at an early age; I guess around four, maybe five years of age. Of course at that age I believed that your mind just starts to develop, and the imagination begins towards the inner part of the thinking stage and the thoughts of excitement.

Therressa is also thinking that life is like a camera lens looking though a glass window and not knowing where or how to begin, however, you will be surprised that in some instances I can reflect voluntarily episodes from recent or later years and describe what could be at the end. So the thinking is of course a special secret between yourself and how you got there, or maybe, where you want to go in this magnificent universe for future years to come.

- *'Yes,' Millardd says, I believe you could be right in thinking that way. Quite frankly, I never considered it to be from my point of view especially as I am also a professional Journalist but in a different environment!*

While Therressa starts thinking way back when she was in kindergarten, all the routine and regulations that came with the territory as I recall them, such as morning activities, then a nap in the afternoon, but most of all I used to love the person that narrated all sorts of children's stories. Such a fantasy of pure imagination! Such a unique process in developing independent thoughts of my own!

But, for me at the age of four, I attended a privileged school dedicated to those who have gifts or talents of some kind, like myself in creative and imaginative dreams. It was recognized by my father who pursued this possibility of early development.

I certainly was very privileged and I liked going to that kindergarten school each day and learning different things, and of course being with other children of my own age but, I also liked to return home, as I was always feeling tired and missed my space in playing and dressing up my dolls.

I spent endless hours changing dresses and combing my dolls hair so that I could display them in my imaginative 'News Agency Shop'. I would lay out all the magazines and newspapers that my mother or father left behind in the lounge room. It was a good display and I would be encouraged to take money from a purchase that my brother or sister gave to me. I think it was at that time I began to understand the value of money and appreciate the link between communication aspects too.

As my journey unfolds there are episodes of laughter, sadness, and of course happiness. In which order they fell into place I can't really examine or identify the place or even the feeling, anyway let's move on and find out, shall we?

- *Therressa reminds Millardd, let's not forsake, or forget the power of thought!*

As a consequence, Therressa, what pastime activities did you like doing, and what made you feel comfortable or happy?

Thanks Millardd, I am glad that you brought that up as it never seems to leave me in my thoughts as a child that is, sitting in the garden, reading a book that I have just obtained from our local library, or exploring the blackberry or strawberry bushes, planted by my father. There were certainly an abundance to be picked and of course, I would enjoy the wonderful flavours while sitting watching my father feed the chickens in their coop and collecting their eggs.

I guess from my point of view, it was a sort of learning process and meditation at the same time with someone I had immense love and trust in, that was my father. I also used to help in planting some seeds to become in later years wonderful bushes of fruit or just pretty flowers such as daisies, you might even start to talk to them and ask them some questions about a course of action or promises you want to make, of course they can't answer you back but, it's like talking to yourself, wishing that there was no one behind you listening to this private conversation, how embarrassing!

Once, I had a very loveable large dog called "Pipa," we nicknamed her as 'Pip', she would just sit by me as I would talk and talk forever about events or situations and it seemed, until she was disturbed by somewhat surprise of her own, that is to do his only private business by herself, "YES" alleviate herself. Nonetheless she always returned to my side.

We started to train her and discipline her in a doggy fashion, as an example, when we stopped at a cross road we would say, "SIT." so she would stand and the opposite of "STAND, " she would sit, a very funny situation and embarrassing when she met other familiar dogs in training exercises.

Unfortunately the loss of her always upset my routine and unashamedly went radical. To this day I always give thanks to the heaven of animal kingdom that I was blessed, almost seventeen years of friendship from a beautiful loving and loyal dog.

If you start to think that's insane well you might be right, but it's good to speak out aloud to yourself sometimes as this will maintain special moments for you. Maybe it could be taken as a sentimental kind of happiness, or sadness, perhaps listening to a piece of music that falls back on a time that took place in the past.

I was also lucky to live near a railway track where trains carrying cargo of some sort, I think it was coal as all families had fireplaces for heating in those days. The track was at the end of the garden and we, that is my sister and brother, close enough at the same age, would collect the train numbers and register the exact times when they passed, it seemed such fun until it was interrupted by the call of my mother instructing us to wash our hands, and that dinner was ready to be served, they call it lunch now, a bit more posh or sophisticated, anyway we were obliged to obey her for fear of going hungry, which sometimes happened.

The value of these experiences obeyed and, of course coupled with this routine performance, made a foundation for me and disciplined me for unforeseen mistakes or successes undertaken.

The garden was a place where I found solace and solitude which allowed me some space, away from the conflict atmospheres within the house as arguments often occurred between my father and mother. It was so atmospherically disturbing, and just to escape into a paradox of my own was very soothing. I developed and learned quickly and recognized that I could take a paradigm shift in my life, not just understanding but also taking steps of action that became real for me in later years.

Therressa, thinking back between each memory as a child, what did you want?

What were the imperative motives or expression, intrusions of your development?

Was it doubt within yourself?

Oh, that is a combination of hard questions Millardd!

Maybe, I was looking for some peace or recognition as an individual and not a comparison to my sister or brother, and yes I did feel inferior against them, but I had no doubt in my mind that I could rectify this as years passed by.

I remember one time at an early age that I burst into the kitchen to tell my mother of some good news that my teacher in my class of English

H 2348 929

and History had given me, such positive results from exams taken.

So I rushed home only to be scolded by my mother as my brother was in the kitchen with his friends talking to her and was not allowed to be interrupted. I was chastised for this interruption. I felt ashamed and sad at this, so instead I approached my father, who was so delighted and hugged me with a worthwhile smile and congratulations. He took all the sadness away from me and I learned never ever would I do this again. I must please and obey my mother's knowledge and concerns.

It meant so much to me at least I thought someone cared. I wanted most of all to be independent unlike siblings a sister and a brother both older than me and to be recognized for me only and the achievements that took place in later years. We used to travel a lot not just within the parameters of England UK, but most of all

overseas, such as Paris, Chicago USA, Canada, Spain, Italy, in fact most of all Europe.

Italy would have had to be my favourite place as we frequented it at least a couple of times a year, within school holidays. It was a beautiful place where you could do anything you liked, either, going to the beach or shopping; at that time we all had bicycles to browse around the narrow city squares and indulge in unique cafés and find the finest selection of various foods.

I had an Aunt, called Theresa who lived there, hence my given name, but spelt differently. Unfortunately she was widowed at a very early age, I think around her late twenties; however she just adored living in Rome the capital of Italy, and declared never to leave it and return back to England. She says, in the heart of Rome a most fascinating place, you can enjoy and escape into an atmosphere with other tourists or even the locals for that matter, and have a sense of belonging. It was then that I began to develop a mind of my own that at least no one could touch or intrude upon.

I loved any part of history. It was ideal for me to take in all of the Italian historic buildings, paintings of Bernini, Michael Angelo and of course the architecture of the centuries gone past. I often thought about what it could have been like in those days, very primitive, yet exciting, we call it the Roman days.

We also travelled to Paris, France many times as it was very close to the UK. Sometimes we travelled by ship, but most of the time we went by plane, I also wanted to be true to myself and grow into a personality and form a character that would mould me to life itself, whether it is true or false, perhaps the answer that I wished for is the truth, and to discover who I will be when I grow into a mature age.

Your question to me Millardd, about having any doubts in my mind!

They were eventually faded into positive reactions, so the answer is, No; I never doubted myself in any achievements. I had all the motivation I could muster up, dedicated to start a project at the beginning and finish at the end. All of my projects accomplished were worthwhile and the achievements satisfied my thirst of learning more with a great deal of zest and courage.

I love working towards a deadline and pressure belt. It makes me more determined and inspired to achieve the end result.

Discipline is a key factor to the end results and is a good virtue of mine. I take my work very seriously to the point of being extremely pedantic and precise. I certainly feel in full control of any project, whether it being an interview or writing a certain article. Negativity does not exist in my line of work but, a practical approach to positivity remains secure. I am always ready to dedicate my time and effort for the success of any project.

- *It seems to me that it was exciting and, at the same time challenging, don't you think so Therressa?*

But Millardd, please call me Rressa, most others call me Tess, but, I prefer Rressa, as it seems a little more elegant and quaint at the same time, Therressa is too formal, and it inhibits my thoughts.

Yes, there were many challenges like all children have a need to learn, the faster the better so that it would become exciting. At times I felt uncomfortable about myself, believe it or not, as at the early age of seven or eight, I did not recognize or believe I had an opinion in myself at all. I always considered from my point of view a failure looking up to my other siblings, or worst still the expectations of my parents wishes.

I certainly was not pretty like my sister or academic like my brother. To him everything he did was so easy as if no excitement was establishing, maybe, he was bored, well to my mind that is a poor attitude to take; whereas me it sometimes got very intense as my ultimate goals were of achievements in the proper manner to take the bull by the horns and go straight into it.

My sister was very attractive and charmed almost anyone who came near to her. She was a very good conversationalist but never a good listener even though she did most of the talking and never even remembers any facts of the conversations that took place within a crowd or group of people. It was just pure gossip amongst friends.

To me that is sad because, I believe when you listen to others you develop your own personality and style and that of course makes you an individual, however she had this appeal so obvious to others, but for me I was a little bit shy. You see I liked being in my own space, it gave me sanctity, solace and peace of mind not to mention the ability to enjoy if you like the pleasure of adversity, call it selfish but in reality it was a comfortable atmosphere and that belonged only to me.

I cared for other people more than myself and wanted to help them, give support in times of crisis, such as carrying the raincoats or other gear on my shoulders for my friends at school.

I myself loved it, out of pure satisfaction, and considered it not as a duty, and it was not within its boundaries but, what is that I believed in was an automatic reaction. I took great pride in myself in giving a helping hand, until I was scolded for this act of charity from my mother. She thought I was weak and that I had no stamina to stand up for myself. How unfortunate I thought this to be! I also felt that I was forced into becoming someone academic who in time destroyed part of my creativity and imagination.

It wasn't considered as a favour of some kind but, to me a gesture of friendship and goodwill to helping others.

I was made to feel ashamed of myself just because of this silly act and it gave way to my despair, so in time I had to convince myself that this has got to stop, but it was always hard for me, nonetheless, I tried to figure out a solution later on, and thank goodness I did solve this dilemma in time later on in life.

But, I was not defeated or ashamed at that moment it was between being able to learn and recognize faults of myself or even penetrating enquiries from others, not to mention the fact that I was also becoming quite proud of myself.

What was it like in your later school days, and more importantly, what subjects were of interest to you?

It was a wonderful stage of my life and yet sometimes in parts became difficult together, with pressure and the fear and sadness of failure.

I never wanted to leave school but, when I reached the mature age of leaving Primary School aged 11 years. It felt very stage and obscure. So many occurrences took place, many more studies to learn, more discipline. I remember one occurrence that took place in my high school was a real tragedy, you see a boy no younger than myself about fifteen years of age committed suicide, no fault of his own, he just fell in love with a male teacher and fell to his death from a second storey school building, just because, he was in love with this teacher a very sad affair!

Beyond that, it became a situation that was expressed with anxiety and, fear of the move and anticipation that leaves you with an impact on life itself.

My favorite subjects were English and History. I liked English because words to me had so much meaning and expression of communication. I studied most of the definitions used in other books to identify a true sense of what the writer was explaining between each sentence or paragraph, very interesting and giving a more detail of the story behind each word documented.

History was also a means of describing hardship and courage, self strength if you like maybe to become part of the history one day in looking back on my previous documented articles and books.

It wasn't just the History of England but all of the other countries that fell into a realm of great people, such as American history of Jefferson and Kennedy, Italian history of ancient methods and rules of empires and wealth of accumulated artifacts, such as paintings by Bernini, Michael Angelo and of course all the battles that were fought with brave men and courage to combat enemies.

However, I also liked mathematics, I wasn't particular good at it, but I was intrigued by the equations and calculation methods. Surprisingly later in years I became an Accountant which was not planned as a career but, at that time when I was about twenty five years old I found myself working in a well known Bank for many years, but my heart laid firmly in other career choices that I took on later.

- *But this was to be only a temporary career, yes!*

Journalism was a future choice because I love to mix with people and to find out their interests and unique ways of their lifestyle.

I had the chance to join a large international advertising company and to qualify and upgrade, of course through dedicated study, and eventually become a Journalist.

- *Perhaps we can interrupt this career journey and focus on a more social scene!*

I know that you like music, so what type of music did you enjoy in the past and maybe still enjoy today Rressa?

I was brought up in the atmosphere of music, my mother loved jazz, my father a bit more contemporary, but I enjoyed both including classical music, but of course in the heart of the 'Sixties', it was, Rock and Roll, the Beatles, Rolling Stones, in fact my much-loved music was always the soul music such as Marvin Gaye, Dianna Ross and the Supremes.

When visiting the record stores they were full with all the recent records, no such thing as the CD, it was vinyl; we listened within the booths available to the music and enjoyed every moment and, then went home to have a bath that was on every Saturday evenings.

I also like the classical music such as Bach, Vivaldi and most others. They have a very calming effect on the mind and especially when you are concentrating on combining research findings and documenting the information into an article or recording interviews.

Give me an idea of what type, if any, routine did you fall into when you were younger after leaving school perhaps?

The weekends basically fell into a routine by its self. A combination of chores, dancing to music while dusting or vacuuming the house, changing bed linen a thorough tidy and clean up day was indeed a Saturday routine.

Sundays were a little bit different as I remembered those moments in front of the mirror getting all dressed up ready for Church Mass. It really turned out to be a meeting place to see boys whose minds were very far from the reason they were there in church, who looked at you instead of paying attention to the spoken gospel being narrated by the Minister.

My Sister, Mother and, of course myself would make sure that we were dressed in the latest style of clothes, new dresses and hats to match the outfit, however shoes was a dilemma because of the tight and high fitting – when I think about it now I walked very slowly in fear of falling onto the pavement in the street, because they were stilettos and very high, but extremely elegant - such pain to suffer in the name of vanity.

The rest of the week that is Monday to Friday was also a normal routine. I used to get up in the mornings before anyone else, except, my Father, who made tea and a slice of toast for me after I had washed and dressed for work. Sometimes we would walk to where my father worked which was in a very exclusive factory of cosmetics, in fact, Elizabeth Arden. He used to bring home many samples of perfume and other cosmetic products as I, at that time, had very bad acne on my skin, so he helped me with this terrible disease and, fortunately repaired all the scars, especially on the face.

He was the most generous and very thoughtful kind man. Our walk was only a couple of miles (kilometers) then I would catch a train right into the heart of London City. All employees had what they called a locker for changing clothes or storing makeup.

We had a uniform of a white blouse and black skirt this was compulsory. We started on the floor ready to oblige customers of their purchases at nine am then finished at six pm. My return home would take only twenty minutes and ready for the evening meal just in time.

So Rressa, how did these recollections become tomorrow from yesteryears?

Well I can remember all of the jealousies and the hatred amongst the students in high school, fulfilling their academic ambitions or career pathways, you see, every Monday was a math's lesson and after the class ended, the assembly hall was used as a dance practice time but, on some occasions I was retained after school, either because of lack of attention within the class room or perhaps the laziness of not doing my homework on time.

However watching all the dancing groups in the hall gave way to jealousy but, I still enjoyed my Math's classes and, I was nearly top of the class when it came to the exam results. How I wished those years were fulfilled with success instead of failure.

Returning home from classes dinner was prepared by my mother which consisted mainly only of a small piece of ham which was very expensive, and a small salad consisting only of lettuce, tomatoes, celery and, my favourite beetroot, let alone no dressing or perhaps a drop of salad cream.

For supper we used to toast a piece of bread with maybe some baked beans, very delicious and tasty not to mention filling before we retired for the evening into bed, as we really had to get up quite early especially when I started work. The transport system was very unreliable so many times I would walk to work which would perhaps be as long as two or three miles in distance.

Today, I am so glad of that distant walk because, it kept me fit even at the age of Sixteen, I did not realize the circumstances of being fit or doing exercise like they exist today, it was a necessity not a luxury but a duty of getting to work on time.

Did you ever render yourself lucky at home or even when you started in the workplace and, how difficult was it Rressa to get yourself a position in those days?

I was so lucky and proud to have been given the opportunity to have a job especially in the sixties. I started as a window dresser, and liked it very much, however I had some irritations as my concentration in designing windows to suit the style, or theme of the weeks specials because of the passerby's in the street would stand and watch me dressing the window models; how frustrating!

For them it seemed amusing but for me it was my job to be creative and responsible for this task. The school boys were the worst as they used to whistle and make fun but, thank goodness, I paid little attention to them.

In my mind I wanted to develop this career within a larger organization such as a department store in the heart of London.

Fortunately, my success as a window dresser was approved upon a very lengthy interview with the department store called Selfridges. I felt so excited and proud of my achievement to get the opportunity and never looked back. I developed more skills in design and knowledge of customer enticement through a display of glass windows.

If you ask me what my other ambition in a career choice would be, I would answer to become, a Flight Attendant, in those days, they called it a glorified waitress on an airline, but for me it was the most important and no occupation that anyone could imagine could exist.

I remember when I went to Chicago the first time to visit one of my Aunts, Sophia she was called and lived downtown as they call it. Her house was really located right in the centre of the large city amongst the tree blossomed avenues and close nearby to the famous Michigan Lake. I only recognized the power of money, going shopping in Marshall Fields, the most famous department store in the USA, but my research provided me about the realities and the hardship of the success of this department store from way back as far as the revolutionary of Mr. Selfridge; how quaint!

My traveling extended also into Canada, Montreal, in fact, a very fascinating city with a concept that all house roofs were to be painted in green. They recognized this feature as a symbol of hope. A one-time Uncle on my mother's side called John, what an easy name to remember, he invited me to stay for a few weeks. I could not ski but what brought back the memories was the fact that he invited me within his family; at last I knew that I had some cousins or relationships.

He was a very talented man, an Architect by profession but also had a passion for painting, landscapes were his specialty, and they were exhibited through museums and art galleries.

He was very strict in himself and was supportive of any mishaps mistakenly intuitive. He was a delight, very much the extravagance entrepreneur, a villa in the Swiss Alps and a mansion the size to me of a palace, but he was a special Uncle and favoured of most of all the wisdom of life.

I spend nearly two months with him and their three young children who were delightful, with no inhibitions on just caring parents and of course the handful of festive food, who could not resist that!

It seemed so far away for me to believe that I was recognized as the poor relative and yet he believed in me with all the heart-to-heart chats he had enormously encouraged me to write down in my own diary circumstances and situations, a very much free conversationalist.

The only drawback I had was the dialect language even though they spoke American but also the French language, personally I did not like the accent of French and never took it as a subject at school instead I took Latin a beautiful and comprehensive language to me. I considered it to be more romantic with a flow of accentuated expression, I learned the language fluently verbally, and written as time progressed throughout my lifetime and later I married an Italian.

Travelling was such a learning and knowledgeable experience however I knew that I needed to return to England, UK, especially as my father was becoming more incapacitated; you see the lungs have a way of telling the person to relax and to take it easy. Well for him having fought in the war and, had been shot in the chest, as a result had a punctured lung. He could only breathe spasmodically, but needless to say he still loved listening to his music and watching me dance for his own enjoyment. He taught me patience and gave me his full support to encourage me into what I wanted to achieve, whether it be the arts or even academic. By profession he was a Civil Engineer before and during the war travelled to the Middle East and other places on demand from his superiors.

I remember in my high school years he taught me to draw and paint. He showed me the art of imagination through colour and perspective lines. Once he gave me a lesson on facial figure and draw them from numbers, as an example the number four became a nose, the number five the chin, the eyes a combination of a one or a two. He was a true artist and like his cousin had paintings exhibited in churches and, also won a scholarship to paint for a prominent person in the political scene.

- *It seems to me that you were very much favoured by your father!*

Yes, that was a true statement, I think it was my creative ability, my concentration to examine and learn from him. All the encouragement he gave seemed so easy when I applied the skill and knowledge. Hence, if today, he was still alive I am sure he would be very proud of me as I am myself, however without too much of an enormous egoistical character.

On the other hand that is my mother; she was quite different in many senses that, she was a very practical person. She was very defiant in her decision making and, was totally in control of many household chores including budgeting the finances. She was extremely talented in selling and ended up working in one of the most famous department stores in London called Harrods. Throughout her time spent there, she was promoted several times one, becoming a department Manager in ladies wear. Her selling skills were also a contribution to her dignity and meticulous appearances.

At home she taught all her children to be disciplined with the utmost manners especially at the dining table, as an example, it would be asking for permission to leave the table for some reason which was almost like an interrogation. Sometimes we just used to sit at the table in total silence until we were given permission to leave and do school homework or another chore of some kind.

- *So looking back Rressa it seems a pity that this performance if you like, was too rigid!*

It was rigid not all the time, but it taught us manners, respect, and attitude towards the discipline as we grew into adulthood.

My mother was very stoic and never ever appreciated or looked for compliments such as her cooking abilities or having the house neat, clean, and tidy. As mentioned before she was a very practical woman 'take me as you see me,' was her attitude. Shopping days were fundamental of course one has to replenish the pantry and fridge for consumption of food. Her selling abilities came in very handy when bargaining, either with the butcher or dairy shops, she was so confident and I learnt lessons in that just by watching and listening to her verbal words.

I remember one time especially in the butcher shop that I was given the opportunity to shop alone without the company of my mother; no doubt she gave way to trusting me in my judgment.

When I was ordering pieces of meat at the butchers, after skeptical appearance in the show case, I chose some pork piece and was delighted at the outcome and of course the price that came with it.

When I returned home I was rebuked at the disgrace my mother showed upon me, she was indeed disappointed in my selection of meat and asked me to return it. To my utmost embarrassment I did as she instructed, however and lucky for me the butcher did replace the meat when he discovered that I was the daughter of my mother, what an influence her approach was, so precise decision never escaped her, on the contrary she was very well liked for her fortitude towards business people the courage they obtained to run any sort of business.

She also had a gentle side of her that reflected consideration for others in need, either a friendly chat or an errand to take care of for friends or neighbours. She had policies in place to be obeyed and not be taken for granted.

So, yes I considered myself very lucky to have a good home full of encouragement and of course discipline even though it was thoroughly organized, it had to be otherwise we could have gone wild and, 'off the rails', as they call it. I guess the ultimate lesson learned was respect for my parents and relatives, which in today's environment families are so overwhelmingly obligated to the demands of their children.

Not a very good idea to bring up children in this way,they lack for nothing these days, therefore I question myself in thinking, what will they look forward to in their own future lives when they are so used to having their own way and materialistic objects at their hands. Such a shame for them!

- *Millardd say's to Rressa, "I think we should now take a*

small break in order to relax the thoughts playing on your mind and to have some lunch to enjoy the lengthy interview of your early years."

- I must admit that it has passed by so quickly in a short time of four hours and, yes, I am ready for a break then I will continue my memories from the past and present. Nonetheless, not so melancholy or otherwise retribution of failure but surprisingly as I think of what I have revealed to Millardd, it all fits into place until the next journey continues.

INTERLUDE
EARLY RECOLLECTION JOURNEYS

- Millardd had chosen a different office a bit quieter and less formal than the others. We were seated in large high backed chairs, very comfortable and easier to relax. Millardd always carried a large folder clipped with blank paper ready to start a session - plus his enthusiasm was gratifying and made me also ready to continue. He anticipated perhaps another four hours and then another full break at the end of the day.

- So Rressa, let's continue the interview and where we left off from our last session.

I would like to understand or know about your career choice,

was it by chance that you found a career of your choice, or was it by default?

I think it was by chance. My default career of my choice was too far away at that time so, having gained a workplace position earlier in an administration office, this being a large advertising company, gave me a beginning.

It seemed a bit more disappointing, perhaps a change that my chosen career of a Flight Attendant was not available as I was too young. You had to be twenty one years of age and at that time I was only nineteen. Even though I passed all of the exams and a full interview, training was too far away. However, I never gave up as I approached the required age of twenty one, but between those times things had changed and my thoughts began to expand into a more career choice as a qualified Journalistic Reporter.

- *It seems to me that you took on the major opportunity that you recognized in your future career options!*

Yes, I recognized and took the opportunity to become an Assistant Journalist for a local newspaper company, which required the skills and knowledge of listening and then reporting through articles and presentations. For me it came as a surprise because even though I had some experience I did lack presentation skills but it did not alter my decision to join the company as it was a recommendation from a dear friend of mine called Gabriella. This position as Assistant Journalist gave me the gateway to other opportunities that lead me in the direction and the person I have become today, a kind of foundation if you like!

Gabriella was a patron of, and veteran in marketing skills, plus have the ability to win interviewers hearts, very strong qualities in

Journalism. She was from Spain who had migrated to the U K and studied at a well know college north of London to exercise and gain the very well deserved qualification in Journalism. We used to converse to each other in opposite languages her in Italian and me in Spanish it was really good fun.

At the time it seemed quite amusing as other people around us not only understood us but the two languages intercepted by us seemed very appropriately adept. We used to start laughing and teased them enormously out of sheer amusement to ourselves.

She was studying Italian while I at that same time had completed my diploma in the Italian language, that took me nearly four years to complete. I also took a course in the Spanish language, very similar to Italian however the pronunciation was quite different more rustic in voice compared to Italian slightly softer. Anyway I loved both languages and eventually became completely fluent in speaking and writing both languages.

Anyway for a start I had no concept of the skills associated with the learning tools in Marketing to become a qualified Journalist. I started at the writers end, but before long as I undertook the position in a large international advertising company, it was only part time, I found myself really enjoying, not just the work, but the people around me and the knowledge and skills they imparted to me.

I began to examine and study hard at this new knowledge and skill and became very proficient in the recognition of what a great subject. This also lead me into researching abilities that proved to be not just useful but, also in a conversation, it was extremely a skill of opportunities.

- *Of course you must have had a contingency plan in place if this career failed!*

Yes, perhaps a career in accountancy or at least administration, but at that time I felt sure to obtain the career within an airline company.

Because I was studying marketing to become a Journalist I thought it would be an appropriate shift if this also failed.

You see, as mentioned before, I was serious to be independent and have a career and, at the end of the day, I could be proud to have established not only educational qualifications, but also to implement and establish my own future choices.

At that time I certainly had no intention to get married however in those decades if you were not married by the age of eighteen at the latest twenty years old, you were considered to be an old maid, as they used to call it or worse still on the shelf.

- I know that you mentioned previously that you challenged yourself constantly by a learning process of simple steps!

So, what steps did you take in this progress and to pursue your career?

I was only about fourteen years of age when I started planning to break away from all the mundane routine such as school and chores that my mother was constantly reminding me of the importance of household cleanliness. You could think that I was locked up in a prison but it wasn't like that, I just wanted to become more independent and realized, that to cross the threshold into another country so far away from home would satisfy my appetite.

The planning stages took me a couple of years to plan and organize and, to my surprise it was all significant. Perhaps a little more fortitude would have been better to make a greater success of the entire plan; however it held a future of more or less growth towards my life.

When I decided to go to another country for a couple or more years, and experience different cultures and life styles, and of course my ultimate ambition was to learn fluently a different language apart from English. At that time I was studying other languages, Italian and German, both of which I claimed a certificate qualification.

I put my whole heart and soul into understanding and learning the dialect, grammar and, putting sentences together. I was committed to learning at least five words a day and practiced them verbally on a daily basis with other people. The country I chose to further my independence and experiences was Italy. It provided evidence to me that I had made a good decision to live there, however there were milestones, inconveniences and irritations that took me step back and two steps forward. First of all I needed to make sure I obtained a legal visa and secondly I needed to make sure I had good accommodation.

I approached the necessary offices and with much substantiation I applied to become a Nanny. It entailed according to the contract that I would be looking after three children in a very well known prominent household south of Italy called Palermo of Sicily. The mother of this household was a celebrity singer and dancer for an Italian television network. The father was a Professor in Scientific Analysis, a very strong character and well established in his field of expertise.

When I arrived in this family circle it was very overwhelming for me, as I was so used to a big city. It was a beautiful house with the exact furnishings to coincide with the extravagance of the family's professional lives. All three children were very well behaved, so my position was a little easier than I expected. My duties included, bathing the children taking them for walks and most importantly to teach them English on a daily basis. This was essential to provide them with constructive homework and, physical activities plus English language studies.

Tutoring with them was such fun as my Italian accent was not as potent as it should have been but, living there within the people's culture, I took measures to rectify this immediately with much enthusiasm. However I was not perfect and of course made many mistakes in pronunciation and grammar, as some words or emphasis can take on a different meaning. I became very conscious and cautious of this and soon tried my perfection on the children.

I considered myself as a true professional; I felt free from my own home and loved every waking from dawn to dust. Such freedom taught me to be more independent and making relative decisions of my own believing that I was living in another country excited me and gave me courage and confidence; I guess a starting point in believing in myself for the first time without negatives or intrusions that could distract me.

Considering my return to London after my contract had ended – I thought it might be a good idea to become a teacher, or maybe enrolling into college to further my education in Marketing. What a great idea some of my friends advised but it soon over lapped on my everlasting desire to become a Journalist. I knew that I would travel in this profession so I pursued this pathway step by step, learning practical and researching skills, documenting stories or articles I had picked up on the way.

How did you feel Rressa when you first recognized the sensation of this strategic method or plan of yours?

I felt that I had no fear in taking risks or, better still in making my own decisions through negative or positive mistakes, my confidence was indeed growing.

Also, at that time in Italy I did miss the freedom and independence that I acquired productively, so I wrote to one of my Aunties, Sophia, who lived in Chicago, the United States of America, and she invited me to visit her and undertake a small vacation with her.

I had visited my Aunt Sophia on several occasions when I was younger and thoroughly enjoyed her unique company. Lots of conversations and shopping sprees spread over into many famous department stores. It was a real delight to be with her.

She was from my father's side of the family, you might call it a distant relative, but I really benefited from her companionship and the encouragement brought in by her charming charisma.

She took me to nearly every famous department store, such as, Marshall Fields, and Macy's, huge buildings and at that time it was considered very elegant. She, that is Aunt Sophia, was very extravagant and would buy me almost anything, not out of disgraceful circumstance but by offering and revealing gratitude of a welcome gift.

Her large department accommodation comprised of three bedrooms, which included a separate bathroom full of the luxuries that you could imagine, however I never dreamed of taking advantage of her wealth, so I suggested paying my share of rent, she of course dismissed the thought and it was never mentioned again.

Just to sit talking to her which she also loved, and to reminisce about her own life experiences from time to time especially during the nineteen twenties and thirties. She was extremely flamboyant, having guests over for entertaining dinner parties and, all the travels she made considerably beneficial to her professional lifestyle.

Her profession was exclusive Interior Design. Her clients was a mixture of noble and entrepreneurs wanting to lavishly furnish their apartments or houses, as she was very well known and an expert in her intuition techniques and style. At one time I thought I took some of her talented gifts with me and was able to readjust my own talents, either in conversation or artistry qualities.

I considered myself very humble just visiting another country for freedom, however perhaps very boring for her, but no she admired my tenacity, courage, and fortitude nevertheless. She was very well liked by everyone who came in contact with her. Sophia's husband was also very well known, he owned and operated a business in the textile industry, and no wonder that Sophia's wardrobe was full of the most up-to-date garments that she wore with great pride, not showing off but, elegantly dressed with dignity and class.

- *I get the feeling Rressa that your independence or freedom was as equally paramount to you as your career choices!*

Yes it was, it always crept into my plans and schedules however, I never thrust aside any support from other people. I just made my own decision and I know that my Aunt Sophia welcomed that from me. I became very perceptive and reliable, so my contingency plan did work up to a point, and as it grew so did my future goals and confidence in acknowledging these transformations developed.

I thought "yes", I can achieve this and take more risks without any fear of rejection or failure. This does not mean that my ego expanded, on the contrary it was well balanced and controlled without any flattery from others whom I must admit their own egos were non touchable.

What sort of experiences did you gather from all of your positions in the workplace?

Well to begin with, I knew I loved to be around people and enjoy their stories and inter mix within their company.

My confidence increased with every introduction to new people of interest and I would initiate a conversation just by listening to them. Talking and speaking to them provided a sequence of conversation and stories from their own lives.

Of course other experiences did not just rest within conversation skills but, in practical skills such as, typing reports and presentation skills when presenting them to management. For me this was very challenging so once again off I went back to College to learn another skill in establishing success and of course obtain another qualification, you might say it was climbing up the ladder, but for me I really enjoyed all my learning.

- *I understand Rressa that it just wasn't always so serious with study and work.*

Tell me what happened in some occasions within a workplace position?

Well in one of my positions I remember the boss called Albert, a middle aged male, insisted that my name did not suit me so he always called me **ROSE**. I really hated it and tried to ignore him when he called me and, I repeatedly mentioned that this is not my name so don't be so rude. His teasing was increasing amusing for him but very stressful for me. After many months of this, even though I liked the work, it was very courageous of me to forfeit my position and look elsewhere.

Fortunately, there were plenty other positions available, so it wasn't long before I took on a better workplace position, however it did not last very long as the work was really boring. I wanted to increase my status, so I enrolled into an education program to develop my writing and Journalism knowledge plus, improve my chances to develop a more positive career direction.

Why did you choose to become a Journalist and join a magazine company? Was it because you had a career change or maybe the

realization of a future relating to people?

It all happen without any force, a friend of mine mentioned that I had so much patience and listening skills that I should consider going into Journalism. However I really needed to brush up on my presentation skills and be very succinct in my writing knowledge or even practicing my interviewing skills. I did this practice in front of the mirror, can you imagine that talking to yourself at a mirror, but it served its purpose and, I soon developed the confidence and proficiency to ask appropriate questions, learning to understand the correct answers I required for all of my reports and articles and to reach my certain goals.

I took up the challenge in presenting my first report and findings from an interview I did with and engineering company that was heading for a major project and development in the city centre of London. All of a sudden

I found myself in the midst of a presentation room with all the equipment set up for me to address the Managers of my findings through research abilities and reporting back to them my discovery from interviews.

It was an articulate and breathtaking experience, however I was also successful in terms of the Managers concerns, that they were not only listening to my presentation but they also enjoyed it. The satisfaction of this presentation was when the management team accepted the project and, it was finally approved to commence construction within two months time.

Nonetheless, it was very frightening and exciting at the same time. As I was presenting I really felt in control without being over powering to the audience, because I have found that in my life it holds the key to the learning process. It's a natural element to be a little fearful in presenting information to others.

You need to get their trust and, to do that you need not only be observant but, to have a good listening capacity to each question and answer as you translate each.

- *Millardd mentions once again that the session needs to have a break and considered it was enough for the day's interview questioning and answering. We need to retire and perhaps tomorrow commence into a rather more than deeper recollections, but first he decided that a dinner at a very well known hotel and restaurant would be a welcome and satisfaction for both of us.*

- *Millardd looked very excited and content with the*

recorded and documented interview results that Therressa Bouques gave him during the two sessions. He was willing to relax and not expedite the remaining bygone stories until the following day; perhaps midday would be perfect, especially for Therressa Bouques. She must be very tired but also exhilarated by not only having remembered some of the past but placing it into perspective as it is narrative material!.

INTERLUDE
A NOSTALGIC JOURNEY

- *The following day when they met up with each other for another interview session Millardd decides to take a different tactic and begins with another process of latter years when Therressa Bouques decides to socialize more and meet a suitable husband maybe!*

Eventually Rressa you did marry later on, so where did you meet your husband or better still decide even that this person was suitable or compatible for you?

Years went by and of course were examined by others saying, aren't you married yet? "You're leaving it a bit too late." Before you know it, it will be too late. However most of my friends had been married very young and had children. Some of them made mistakes in their own choice and had separated from their husbands soon after.

It was a crazy assumption to take in at first as I was, perhaps, not ready for commitment in this diverse relationship with another person. Sharing my thoughts and love certainly did not cross my mind just when life is starting to fall into place, adventures, experiences and the like. Marriage was certainly not on my agenda at that time because of my other commitments to education. Although I did enjoy male company but as yet hadn't found the right person to spend my entire life with. I needed someone who I could love and stimulate my future goals.

I began to think, how do you fall in love?

Nevertheless, you can't put a stop on love when it arrives by accident. It's like an addiction that can't be removed as quickly as it began. In spite of this it soon became apparent to me that this person I recently met in a night club of all places, belonged to me, it was like an attachment of enjoyment and amusement all combined together, and I wasn't going to give in and loose him easily as I found him.

In earlier times, I did have a few short term relationships but, none seemed to fit into my busy schedule or worse still there was nothing to compare the compatibilities of these male acquaintances, so eventually they all faded out. I was approaching nearly thirty years old, but I never argued to having misconceptions or doubts of this recent man that I had just met.

From an early age around twenty years old, I knew that I could not bear a child for him because of previous medical reasons. His name was Alex and he was very sympathetic towards the situation but never pondered or thought negatively upon this situation, there are other ways to have children by adoption.

We only had a very short engagement, I think about four months as I didn't believe in prolonging marriage.

Alex was very comforting towards not having a family but, it also meant that I could continue in my chosen career as a Journalist, and he as a top Chef in a major Hotel.

I remember how disappointing it was for my parents, as my sister produced five children and they all distributed equal affection on all of them. Conversely my mother-in-law was so different, the kindest person I have ever encountered, so obliging and caring. The acceptance from her and her family meant so much to me and to be welcomed as a family member into their household was very special to me. She was not at all concerned about seeing other grand children from us but her considerate expression was only that we be happy together, that made her very happy.

Alex was a very caring man and took on the responsibility as a husband very well. However he never interfered with my career or activities, he was just not interested, perhaps to the point of boredom which was a shame because, I could have shared my confidence and securities with him, especially editing articles for publication or presentation practices – but no he was just open to his own affairs and achievements, so I had to concede to my lonely confidence and assuring my own confidence by myself.

He was very domesticated and in later years he told me stories about being in the kitchen watching his mother cooking and preparing meals for the entire family, hence as a result of this he became a very well known Chef who specialized in extraordinary main dishes, as well as famous Italian cuisine. The quality of knowing what ingredients were suitable and of course married with the dish being prepared. He was a very good host to our friends that were often invited to dinners or suppers. Sometimes, especially on week-ends we would have a late breakfast around eleven am instead of lunch. It was made up with all of the usual traditional bacon, sausages, tomatoes, and eggs, together with bottles of champagne and shared this with our closest friends, a most delightful time!

In spite of this the thought of all that housekeeping was miserable for me, quite depressing even though I was immaculate in my cleaning it never attributed to my enthusiasm, but it had to be done, even when I was sent overseas on a project I would call in a cleaner of some kind to help out, but it was never the same as I did it.

What contribution of skills and knowledge did you bring into your marriage and enjoy with your husband?

Perhaps if I look back now the only compatibility was in the kitchen, cooking and preparing dinner parties, we really shared a love of entertaining and of course making sure that our guests enjoys the food and company, apart from that nothing much.

Alex being extremely domesticated like myself, everything had to be neat and tidy and of course clean, which was instilled in me by my own mother at a very early age, around about seven or eight years old. Learning how to make a bed for example, cooking dusting and laundry together with all the other chores to keep the home neat clean and tidy.

My career however always took first place in our relationship and equally his too. I learned a great deal from his cooking and domesticity that I enjoyed working alongside of him in the kitchen preparing meals either for ourselves or if we had dinner parties which became quite frequent.

Later on in our marriage I took a sabbatical from my career work and we ended up going back to Italy to meet and stay a short time with his parents, they were such lovely people who accepted me within minutes. There household was a bit primitive as they lived in a small country village on the outskirts of Florence not far from Rome, approximately one or two hours by car or train.

We stayed with them for about four weeks until we decided to leave and go to Rome and establish a restaurant business a dream for Alex. Our thoughts were to acquire clientele of a different nature such as business people who were always too busy to cook for themselves.

It was definitely going to be an establishment of elegance and unique cuisine. As we grew the restaurant clientele also grew, so we opened a smaller Restaurant-Café, if you like, for younger people with affordable menus. It worked out very well, however the time shifts were difficult as Alex would be working until two or three am in the morning, so I saw him very seldom during the evenings.

In the afternoons, a known fact that in Italy all shops and other outlets closed for a siesta, as they call it about 12 noon until four in the afternoons. This gave me a chance to catch up on meetings and visiting friends. My research had to be precise and delivered appropriately and on time to members of a large marketing-advertising company.

It suited equally for both of us, giving as much space from each other, and to gather rest and relaxation requirements.

Sometimes I used to take a bus into Rome city and invite myself at the bar for an evening drink. I knew all of the staff as I was the one to interview them with the qualification skills and knowledge from the past. We had three major Chef's, four Bar staff, and five Serving staff. The accountant was at the cash desk always to reconcile the profits and make sure that the takings for the day were locked in the safe until banking all monies the following morning.

- *Millardd begins to feel hungry just talking about this section of food and starts to elaborate the importance of sharing this experience about Rressa!*

We rented a small villa in the heart of Rome city for nearly four years. Because Alex was a long time qualified Chef we ultimately owned two Restaurants both being, popular and our clientele were very generous, you might say supported us extremely well. Our food was well known to all of Rome to be the best menu in town, so we did not have to advertise as it was word of mouth that was building up our reputation.

Our main clientele were Bankers, Executives, Male and Female in Corporations such as TV and Radio Producers plus several Directors. They were very easy to talk to and we offered them the highest quality of food and specialized wines and cocktails.

- *Millardd decides it's time to have another break and this time because it was a Friday, we can have the entire weekend off so that Rressa can relax and perhaps write down and consider the best approach to continue the interview journey.*

INTERLUDE
A REMINISCENCE JOURNEY

- *Millardd decides to continue the Monday session by delving into future circumstance, opportunities currently available to me.*

What made you decide to migrate permanently to another country, such as Australia, why not America where you had some distant relatives or other places. And how did you do your research to conduct and compile your research on living standards?

I did a lot of research just to find out what was available in another country such as America and Australia. The available work suited to both of us, the accommodation requirement and the cultural aspects of understanding there lifestyle standards – I guess we would have to adjust ourselves in being a foreigner in another country!

I would have liked to migrate to Canada as I had several uncles from my mother's side living an places such as Montreal and Vancouver.

To tell you the truth, I just wanted so desperately to have a major change from my own family and country and Italy. There seemed to be so many rules and ridged routines, never ending routine, nothing challenging or exiting anymore. So we thought about starting a new life as we were still young and ready for a change in pace and surroundings. So we chose Australia because of it's variety and massive territory.

However the distance from London to Australia was very isolated and desolate. We needed quite frankly to start all over again in some circumstances such as accommodation, new jobs to find, meeting new friends, in other words it was a bit sad to leave a comfortable environment and well established friends and work.

Upon arrival what did you expect, was it so much different to your ideal imagination?

It was a paradigm shift migrating to start a fresh, not a new life but, a different one. It felt strange but also challenging within a different country and culture. To adapt changes had to be made. I needed to learn the rule of conversation what, was suitable and, not suitable, slang words for example how to use them and not offend others. Banking rules, how to open up accounts and obtain cash money, how and when to go shopping.

It suddenly reminds me that the hours of shopping times were very limited, not like the UK or USA when the shops were open until late at night, however here in Australia all shops were opened at 9am and closed at 5pm week days. On Saturdays they opened at 8am and closed at midday and were never opened on a Sunday.

Take away stores really did not exist until the mid eighties and of course took off like a lightening bulb. As referendum and demands from the community came in the entire shopping rules were changed and – yes - they began to open stores and shops until late at night until 6pm and open all day on Saturdays, however Sunday trading was not yet considered until later when the workforce examined the necessity to open on a Sunday for those working long hours and perhaps shift workers together. It certainly was a welcoming rule.

In the early times for us we knew we needed to have a car and luckily I obtained an International vehicle license in USA, UK, and Italy, very useful. Unfortunately Alex never had a license to drive so here in Australia he studied to obtain the very same thing and learn how to drive.

They drove on the opposite side of the road unlike UK and Italy, quite frightening at first but you get used to it eventually.

One major experience that we discovered was entertaining newly acquainted friends whom we invited for either dinner or supper, and to my immediate surprise they brought along their children, unheard of overseas, it was purely a formal situation. I remember the first time this happened and Alex was so shocked when we saw the children that his only thought was to establish how to serve a meal to these children there were three of them ranging from two to six years old.

Our dinner menu consisted of sophisticated foods and drinks such as appetizers as drinks, food as an Anti- Pasto dish, main as Smoked Salmon, and deserts as soufflés. All the expensive material we were used to cooking back home. Alex managed to provide small dishes of beans on toast with some sausages and of course cool drinks for the children. That meant for me more washing up to be done later after they left.

Surprisingly it all went well being our first entertainment of newly guest in this country. We really had a very good laugh at it all when they left, admittedly at a late time close to midnight.

That was a real lesson we learnt and from that day forward we always expected children to come with them.

It seemed that everyone had a car and a house which apparently was a cultural thing. I was lucky because I already had a driver's license, but my husband no.

The question here was, how do you get a car and from whom? We became acquainted fortunately with a couple who were not married but were living together in a long time relationship, he was a car salesman, and the girl was a receptionist in a real estate agency. As soon as they discovered our dilemma it took no time to obtain a second-hand car. It was in good condition and to this day I really loved that car, it took me everywhere around about town and into the country side.

Eventually later-on Alex obtained his own driving license. Coming from a large city the atmosphere seemed very provincial, not too many shops and certainly the rules on opening hours were very strict, such as trading was only a half a day on a Saturday and there was no trading hours on Sundays except the Public Houses, that is the local pubs were opened at midday and closed mid afternoon.

The social life was limited, being new to the country and not understanding the culture, but of course it did not stop us enjoying ourselves. We went for long walks and watched people on the beach. We also visited as many local attractions, one being the major Cathedral in the city, a glorious monument of good architecture design.

How did you find a suitable position in the workplace?

I was very fortunate because a friend of my brothers back home in London came to visit and suggested that I pay a visit to his father's office upon arrival, in which I did a few weeks later. It was a strange interview and here in Australia it's important to know someone rather than produce all qualifications in order to get a job position.

It seemed a really great position however the requirements considered a great deal of ambition (which I already had that together with enthusiasm). It was an Assistant Accountancy position with a great deal of responsibility.

End of month documents had to be presented in a fashion that convey the status of the business and that really frightened me as I was a little bit shy and had no experience with presentation skill, but as time passed by I took the courage to learn and provide these skills effectively. I went to a Technical and Educational College and studied for a diploma in accountancy, there I go again I thought more learning and accomplishments, it was in my nature and it showed in my persona as well with friends we made progressing qualifications and is still a welcoming ambition of mine.

But I missed so terribly the marketing and Journalism work. I started to investigate opportunities for me to enter an enterprise consisting of my already skills and qualifications in this field. I ultimately found a very good position although it was only part-time work it was at least a start to establish contacts and to cultivate the Australian way of communications. It was exciting for me to know that my endeavour's in the past never went to waste.

So Rressa, while you obtained a position and were studying at the same time, what type of work did your husband obtain and accomplish?

Unfortunately it was very difficult for him as he had not cultivated the English language to perfection and at that time did not qualify or be recognized in this country as a qualified Chef. His profession was in hospitality, but it seemed that the only way he could get a position was to return back to college and really start all over again which would take about four or five years to complete. It felt such a shame as he was extremely qualified a seven year qualification and experience of more than twenty years.

Two things stood in the way, one being the cost of the course, and obtaining a qualification in the English language. He would have had to take more exams, the question was, "was it worth it", or should he just do some laboring work to get started. It was almost nearly eight months until he found work and was also considering going back to Europe.

What about accommodation, where did you find were to stay?

It was only by chance that we were passing a Real Estate Agency and when we went inside we were advised that a place was on the market for rent, quite a reasonable priced accommodation and better still it was right in the central part of the city, so I had no transport costs as I could walk to work which suited me because I liked to keep healthy and fit.

We moved in within a week of arriving and it was such a pleasure viewing the river just outside the main window of the small apartment.

We remained in this apartment for over eighteen months that gave us a chance to save our money and place a deposit on a house. The house was in a very good location small with three bedrooms and one bathroom, plenty for two people and not too distant from our working positions. We travelled to work by public transport, very convenient and suitable for our needs.

Do you remember the funniest or maybe strange workplace positions you had in Australia?

To tell the truth I had a few, one in particular was in a large manufacturing company were one of the colleagues would have tantrums and bang on the internal glass partitioning, then one day she broke out into a fury and, for me that was ridiculously dangerous so I left within the week.

Another time was when I was to just serve tea or coffee (how boring not to mention the dress code, it had to be completely black including stockings and shoes). I felt each day suffocating in this atmosphere of pretentious moods and that I was getting ready each morning seemed like going to a funeral and was very depressing.

Another position was that on my first day arriving on time and neatly dressed for the day the boss called me in and said that I could sit in a private corner and read the paper or magazine to fill in my time as they were not very busy.

At the end of the day he asked me what I did all day as he had had some complaints from customers – which I never saw any – what complaints I said, you requested me to sit in the corner and read. Of course I left in laughter and not despair.

When I gave in my notice the boss mentioned – why are you leaving, it's so peaceful here, exactly I thought. So it meant that I was on the search again or maybe just take a small break to organize my mind and go straight into the field of my professional career approach as a qualified Journalist.

I was successful and found a really good position in an advertising company specializing in unique products and interviewing people off the street about buying these various products. It was great fun and of course the opportunity to gain more experience, I lasted nearly eight years with the company leading me into a promotional position as top Journalist.

- *Millardd is so full of satisfaction and successful results from this interview with Rressa that he really doesn't want to stop or interrupt the memories of Rressa's lifetime journey, but he knows that he needs to put all the pieces together and of course let Rressa have a break. He decided to take a* short break in the afternoon and continue in pursuit of current issues of Rressa's journey so he mentions that we can continue in the afternoon until late and perhaps finalize the interview findings.

INTERLUDE
A BOUYANT JOURNEY

- Once again after a few hours break we continued to explore the memories and to conclude the resulting effects that have, not only inspired Millardd, or better still has made Rressa more satisfied and encouraged by the outcomes.

What plans did you make for your retirement that is if you want to retire from the workforce and expect everything would become a little more of freedom?

I guess looking back I did not really have any definite plans, such as the provision of enough money to enjoy my life as it continues to do at the moment, even though I was renowned to be a bit frugal and careful with money.

Today, I have a beautiful home with most luxuries and the value of the property is substantially good. I thought I would like to go free-lance into Journalism, so I approached many companies that would take me on. It proved to be a satisfying option on both sides, freedom, and independence for me and for the company equally an opportunity to keep costs down.

However it sometimes feels empty. I thought about doing some voluntary work as well as my free-lance work, at least I could meet some different people in need of just an occasional visit and chat.

That's me always, some kind of loss, in fact, I felt quite lonely at times, and can you imagine that? Most people would be delighted to stay at home relax and wake up in the mornings late, doing a bit of gardening, cleaning, reading the newspaper, or even watch TV.

I myself would always read or write at this time, it became a habit of mine, when the mind has rested during the night and only by virtue of my passion to have this skill and also to acquire and learn new ideas, such as new recipes, looking at biographies of other famous people how they muddled through without their talent which fades away by age.

So how did you become a professional Writer and Author in a particular field of interest to you? What ideas fell into place at the start of your first book published?

Writing my own books gave me such peace and tranquility, but I would never rush into them. They came together with many years of experiences and of course I had to prepare and edit all of my articles from interviews conducted.

It was a whole new experience for me, a step by step process, not just by writing the books but getting them published was very critical. Understanding the requirements and laws on copyright procedures, very daunting and, exciting at the same time. I was on edge all the time from my first book being published, but fortunately I had researched all publishers and found one that was suitably unique and professional.

The only drawback was the cost of the publication as I did all of my own editing otherwise it would cost me a fortune; nevertheless I managed to continue to publish other books, more of the kind of inspiringly topics and not novel subjects.

The impact it gave me was tremendous, it not only inspired me to publish more books, but feedback from friends were the ultimate compliments one could ever imagine. To see the finished product was very tearful and a remembrance of how much effort I had put into the finished book.

- *Instead of Millardd suggesting to Therressa Bouques to take a break, he says, "let's have lunch together", inthatwayitwould be a different atmosphere more comfortable and relaxing.*

- *So, Rressa agrees that it sounds a perfect way to conclude and finalize the documented interview.*

INTERLUDE
A CULMINATION JOURNEY

- *Starting the interview over lunch did seem more relaxed so, Millardd continued to bring himself more up to date with Rressa's current issues on career, lifestyle, and perhaps prospects for the future!*

So where to from now on Rressa, will you do more travelling or publish new books, or just sit back and take in the marvelous experience, skills, and knowledge accumulated throughout your lifetime of becoming a world class Journalist, which is recognized all over the world over the past 70 years?

I certainly will not Stop travelling or writing, but, perhaps to challenge myself into writing screenplays or to some extent narrative storyline material. You see words are very important to me, it is a way of expression as you read them, you can get the big picture and put yourself within that picture with some imagination it's a pretend thing, but most of all a very well worthwhile challenge.

Some people say that it is a waste of time reading and writing plus being boring, that's because they haven't learned the craft of imagination and of course you need space and time to absorb what the writer is writing about, learning the theme of the novel or documentary. It's ok to watch a film by a writer who has before written the book but, it's not the same as reading the book. In a film there is no imagination, emotion, thrills. Instead by reading the book it plays upon the emotions of what will happen next as you turn each page.

So where do we leave off this wonderful experience that I have had by your documented interview Millardd? I have thoroughly enjoyed tracing back moments in my life whether they were sad, happy or exiting moments, including all the opportunities and risks that I have taken over the years.

- *Millardd now knows that the ending of the interview is near reaching the final stages and wishes to take a day or two break to finalize the recording and documenting the results ready for broadcasting in later weeks to come!*

INTERLUDE

FULLFILMENT AND SATISFACTION

- *Asweapproachtheconclusion of this interview Millardd asks Rressa, 'as to what parts would you consider being the most important parts of revealing your past memories?*

I must say that the time has really passed so quickly when you portray and remember past experiences that reflect a lifetime journey over three or four decades, however I must admit that the entire interview has been part of this experience and of course without your own experience.

Millardd, it has allowed me to continue my future with greater stamina and enthusiasm.

There will always be elements that will not entirely satisfy me or maybe the fulfillment of both successes and challenges to achieve and move on to the next project. As a matter of fact I have been commissioned to research and document, of course interview, a star celebrity in the music industry which I am very excited about. I have engaged some of my colleagues to join me in as much discussion with this celebrity and our schedule will fit into it perfectly in the next coming weeks.

- *But I remember you saying that you might consider retiring and take a little time off, is that going to happen?*

No, I earnestly hope not, but for now I want to thank you Millardd for allowing me to bring out some important parts of my memories and to all the audiences, and hope that this documentary will carry some thoughts to others who may have experienced these events.

- *Millardd says, Rressa it was a most enjoyable experience for me and I will proceed with my intentions to be on schedule for the TV shot as promised coming up in a matter of weeks time.*

I hope to meet up with you again Rressa for another interesting Documentary Interview. In the meantime keep enthusiastic and confident, Bye, Bye for now.

GOOD LUCK!

CIRCULATING STOCK

BLOCK LOAN

5 - JUL 2017   WD 30/7/24

9 781514 446287